ATLIN BLUE *and* MISS SCARLET

Story by Emily Grace Willis

Pictures by Courtenay Birdsall Clifford

Lynn Canal Publishing

Skagway, Alaska

Atlin Blue and Miss Scarlet

Copies may be ordered from:

Lynn Canal Publishing

at

www.skagwaybooks.com

or

Skaguay News Depot & Books direct line: 1-907-983-3354

PO Box 498-LCP, Skagway, AK 99840

ISBN: 978-0-945284-13-0

Distributed outside Skagway, Alaska by Epicenter Press in the USA and by PR Distributing in the Yukon/Canada

Printed in the United States of America

For the Green Thumb in all of us.

And to Yonder and Sage, we love you!

There is a land where steep mountains are capped with snow, where boulders shoulder deep layers of green moss, and where rolling ocean waves are a playground for birds, salmon, seals and whales. In this land, once upon a time, lived a boy named Atlin Blue who was a budding gardener.

As spring arrived to his hometown in the southern reaches of Alaska, Atlin Blue and his mom eagerly anticipated the planting season. A few months earlier they had started vegetable, herb and flower seeds in their mountainside home, and now it was time to transplant them outside. When a string of warmer, yet cloudy days was forecast, they took the healthy green starts and packages of seeds down to the Community Garden.

Now it must be said that Atlin Blue absolutely LOVED carrots! They were his favorite vegetable, especially fresh out of the garden! So he got to work carefully planting the carrot seeds one inch apart in neat rows.

Meanwhile, his mom transplanted their starts of broccoli, kale, cabbage, lettuce, swiss chard, oregano, thyme, calendulas and violas. Then they direct seeded the spinach, radishes, beets and cilantro. Last but not least were the baby potato tubers that had to be buried and labeled.

"Whew!" Atlin Blue exclaimed wiping the soil from his brow. Then, filling the watering can and adding compost tea they had made at home, he watered all the newly planted babies. As he did, he made a silent wish: *I wish you all a happy living that makes you grow and grow and grow.*

Over the next few weeks they tended their plots with care. They added seaweed and compost alongside the growing plants. They weeded out crab grass and harvested horsetail and dandelions. The bright Alaskan sun shone strong and the light rains that fell were greeted happily by the plants. By June the radishes and lettuces were ready for fresh salad and the cabbages were well on their way.

Atlin Blue and his family were going on a vacation to visit his grandparents in the Lower 48, leaving their beds in the care of fellow Community Gardeners. On the way to the ferry that would take them south, they stopped by the garden to give their plant friends a thorough watering. As they were getting back in the car, Atlin Blue called out, "Have a happy living! Take care! We'll see you soon!" Then he shut the door and they pulled away before he could hear the soft rustling of the garden's response.

That soft rustling was in fact the plants chattering amongst themselves. Yes, plants can talk to each other. They are all connected through their shared soil and air. We don't always hear them, but sometimes, if you listen hard, you can catch a whisper here or there.

"Wait, where are they going?" asked Mrs. Ruby Ball Cabbage, "And what do you think he meant by 'have a happy living?' "

"They're supposed to visit us every day! Who will water us? I'm a lettuce green! I'm always thirsty!" wailed Tango with a shimmy of his leaves.

"And who will hum to us and whisper encouraging words? I'll miss that," Mr. Dino Kale said wistfully.

"They've helped us grow by keeping those pesky grasses out of our way. What if the grasses come back?" moaned Ya Ya Carrot.

"Now, now," chided Miss Swiss Chard, "I'm sure they're not gone for good. Atlin Blue did say he'd see us soon."

"Maybe we can see where they're going. Can anyone see? Let's try," Sage Lynn suggested. The whole garden shook with the effort of everyone digging in with their roots and stretching and growing with all their might towards the sky. Managing to merely bump into one another, they soon realized that if they all began to grow to great size, they'd run out of room in their beds.

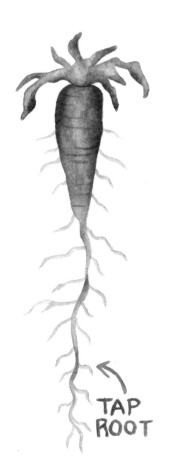

TAP ROOT

"We've got it," sang a chorus of Calendulas, "Let's have one of the carrots grow tall. Their deep tap root will anchor them in so they can reach high enough to see over the mountains."

"I think Miss Scarlet Nantes should be the one," proposed Cosmic Purple. "She grows such a long root that it would be easy to hold her top high."

"Yes, a more dependable carrot you couldn't ask for," added Sir Oxheart. "What do you say, Miss Scarlet?"

One of the shyest carrots in the bunch, Miss Scarlet blushed an even deeper orange, but agreed to give it a try. She did miss Atlin Blue already. She stretched her root hairs farther and deeper than she thought possible. She focused on gathering all the strength she could from the soil. Immediately, she grew a bit taller. The other plants cheered her on, applauding in a rustle of foliage.

A week passed, but it didn't pass unnoticed by the Community Gardeners. Amidst the flourishing plants in Atlin Blue's bed was one wondrously enormous carrot! Miss Scarlet was growing faster and taller every day. Soon she was taller than a fir tree, but that wasn't enough. Still hoping to peer over the mountains in search of Atlin Blue, she reached her root out to the heart of the Skagway River. She drank up its glacial waters at night and skyrocketed toward the sun during the day.

As she grew, Miss Scarlet was mindful of her friends down below. She was a conscientious carrot, after all. She tried to stand very straight as to not block out the sunshine and she brought rich nutrients from way down deep in the soil to share with the rest of the garden.

Eventually she began to gather the attention of the entire town. At first they simply marveled at her size, but they soon had complaints. At times her leafy top obstructed Alaska Street and signs were posted redirecting traffic. Her towering height began to disrupt flight patterns at the nearby airport and the townspeople decided that something had to be done. It was time to harvest the wayward carrot. However, this was easier said than done.

They tried digging with shovels. They tried chopping with axes. They tried slicing with chainsaws. All the tools just bounced off her hearty trunk! They pulled with pickup trucks. They pushed with a bulldozer. They even tried to dislodge it with a helicopter. The mighty carrot would not yield.

Miss Scarlet was getting some help from her friends, you see. All of the other plants reached out, twining their roots with hers, sharing their energy and strength. They knew Miss Scarlet wasn't ready for harvest. They knew she was waiting for Atlin Blue. Of course, fairy magic was helping too. Yes, garden fairies do exist. We don't always see them, but sometimes, if you sit very still, you can catch a flutter of their wings here or there.

Suddenly a loud *Whaah-haah* echoed through town. Miss Scarlet looked out to see that the ferry had docked. "They're back! They're back! Atlin Blue is back!" she shouted. She was relieved. She had been growing and growing for three weeks and she was weary.

Atlin Blue and his parents had heard about events in the garden and rushed to see the wondrously enormous carrot. They were not, however, prepared for what they saw and Atlin Blue dropped his jaw in awe. He slowly approached Miss Scarlet and raised his arms to hug her vast orange trunk.

"Wishes really do come true" he murmured, "you really did grow and grow and grow."

He was not surprised to hear her respond.

She whispered, *I have had a very happy living and now that you are home, I am ready for harvest.*

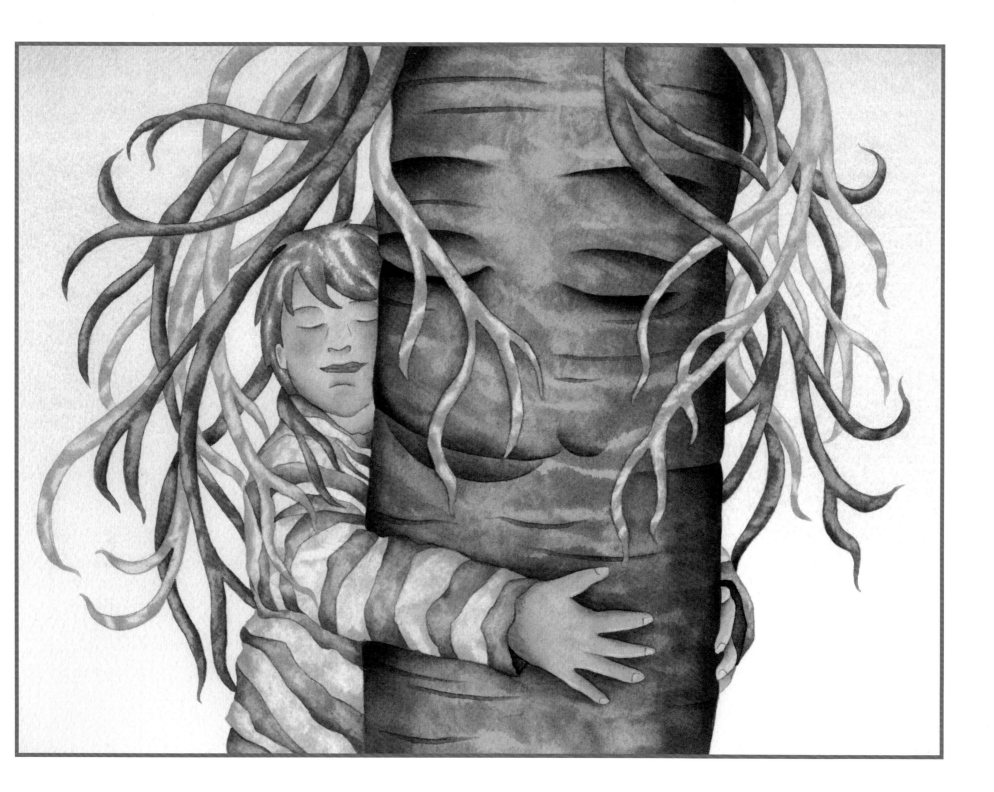

With the slightest heave-ho, he gently freed the carrot from the soil. It toppled smoothly onto Alaska Street (as if cushioned by a thousand fairy wings) for all to behold.

"Come one! Come all! Come share in the harvest!" he cried.

And everyone did come. Even those who had complained before. They came with thoughts of crunchy sweet goodness; of steamed carrots sprinkled with brown sugar; of carrot juice and carrot soup; and, of course, of carrot cake. They came with a thankfulness for nature's generous bounty.

Few of them noticed the soft rustling of the remaining garden plants. The garden was celebrating. They were happy for Miss Scarlet who had fulfilled her destiny. She had been nurtured during her life and now she would nourish others.

Have a happy living!

The End.

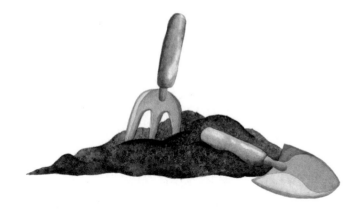